By Christy Webster
Illustrated by Ann Marcellino

A GOLDEN BOOK • NEW YORK

© 2020 MARVEL

All rights reserved. Published in the United States by Golden Books, an imprint of Random House Children's Books, a division of Penguin Random House LLC, 1745 Broadway, New York, NY 10019, and in Canada by Penguin Random House Canada Limited, Toronto. Golden Books, A Golden Book, A Little Golden Book, the G colophon, and the distinctive gold spine are registered trademarks of Penguin Random House LLC.
rhcbooks.com
ISBN 978-0-593-12215-0 (trade) — ISBN 978-0-593-12216-7 (ebook)
Printed in the United States of America
10 9 8 7 6 5 4 3 2 1

The Avenger known as **Black Widow** is the world's greatest spy.

Black Widow's real name is Natasha Romanoff. From a young age, she trained to be **strong** enough to face any challenge . . .

and stealthy enough to sneak up on the sneakiest spies . . . like Yelena Belova and her Hydra goons.

She's fast enough to outpace any villain.

VROOM!

She is a master of martial arts! Her skills
make her a tough match for anyone—
even many opponents at once.

Her **Widow's Bite** bracelets are electrifying.
With them, she can sting any enemy!

Black Widow's past is mysterious because her spy missions were **TOP-SECRET**.

But then she joined the Avengers—a mighty team of Super Heroes! They work together to fight the baddest of the bad guys.

She may not be able to fly, like some heroes, but there's no place too high for Black Widow to reach with her trusty ropes and grappling hooks.

Black Widow is a master of disguise.

She knows how to surprise the bad guys!

She looks out for her teammates, too.

Sometimes Hulk gives her a ride!

Black Widow will fight for
what's right anywhere, anytime.

Black Widow is brave. With her teammates by her side, she always brings the bad guys to justice.

Black Widow and the Avengers make sure to keep the world safe . . .